COMFORT ME WITH APPLES

ALSO BY
CATHERYNNE M. VALENTE

The Labyrinth

Yume No Hon:
The Book of Dreams

The Grass-Cutting Sword

Under in the Mere

Palimpsest

Silently and Very Fast

Deathless

Six-Gun Snow White

Radiance

The Refrigerator Monologues

The Glass Town Game

Space Opera

Mass Effect: Annihilation

Minecraft: The End

The Past Is Red

FAIRYLAND

The Girl Who
Circumnavigated Fairyland
in a Ship of Her Own Making

The Girl Who Fell Beneath
Fairyland and Led
the Revels There

The Girl Who Soared Over
Fairyland and Cut
the Moon in Two

The Boy Who Lost Fairyland

The Girl Who Raced Fairyland
All the Way Home

THE ORPHAN'S TALES

The Orphan's Tales:
In the Night Garden

The Orphan's Tales:
In the Cities of Coin and Spice

A DIRGE FOR
PRESTER JOHN

The Habitation of the Blessed

The Folded World

SHORT FICTION
COLLECTIONS

The Bread We Eat in Dreams

Myths of Origin

The Melancholy of Mechagirl

The Future Is Blue

COMFORT ME WITH APPLES

Catherynne M. Valente

A TOM DOHERTY ASSOCIATES BOOK

NEW YORK

COMFORT ME WITH APPLES

Copyright © 2021 by Catherynne M. Valente

Edited by Jonathan Strahan

A Tordotcom Book
Published by Tom Doherty Associates
120 Broadway
New York, NY 10271

www.tor.com

Tor® is a registered trademark of Macmillan Publishing Group, LLC.

The Library of Congress Cataloging-in-Publication Data
is available upon request.

ISBN 978-1-250-81621-4 (hardcover)
ISBN 978-1-250-81620-7 (ebook)

Our books may be purchased in bulk for promotional,
educational, or business use. Please contact your local bookseller
or the Macmillan Corporate and Premium Sales Department
at 1-800-221-7945, extension 5442, or by email at
MacmillanSpecialMarkets@macmillan.com.

First Edition: October 2021

Printed in the United States of America

0 9 8 7 6 5 4 3 2 1

For Kris, Cylia, and Sarah
Turtles all the way down

COMFORT ME
WITH APPLES

AMBROSIA

The Following Agreement is made this first day of the first month between the members of the Arcadia Gardens Homeowners Association [hereinafter known as "the Association"] and the titleholders of 1 Cedar Drive [hereinafter known as "the Residents" and "the Property," respectively].

The Association, acting through any and whatever such proxies as may be delegated, pursuant to its previously filed Declaration of Intent to Incorporate, in consideration of, and dependent upon, the mutual promises contained herein, desires to appoint the undersigned Residents exclusively to manage the aforementioned Arcadia Gardens property in perpetuity.

Welcome to a new world of luxury living in Arcadia Gardens, an exclusive, upscale gated community! Every thought and care has been taken to provide the ultimate in amenities, privacy, serenity, and, most important, safety for you and yours. Enjoy the benefits of round-the-clock security and access to community gardens and pools. Stroll at your leisure through lovingly designed streets, parks, and common areas. Get to know your friendly neighbors. Most of all, rest soundly knowing the outside world cannot trouble you here.

Your new Arcadia Gardens home boasts the absolute latest in worry-free convenience. Anything you desire can be provided with ease; anything you lack is but a call away. It is important to us that you be happy here. Our goal is pure, sustainable, and entirely self-sufficient contentment, so that you can get on with your vital work without the niggling unpleasantries of everyday dissatisfactions gnawing away at your peace of mind.

In order to create this unique environment of domestic bliss and year-round tranquility, the Association has, in concert with its Board of Directors, set a few simple, easy-to-follow rules. Abide by them, and your new life in Arcadia Gardens will be all anyone could dream of.

1. Should you wish to personalize your dwelling, the following paint colors are acceptable: Virgin White, Eggshell, Purity, First Snow, Antique Porcelain, Morning Star, Fresh Cream, Mother's Milk, and Innocence.
2. No outdoor cooking, ovens, grills, smoke pits, or other open fires.
3. Lawns must be kept to a grass height of not less than one point five (1.5) inches and not more than two (2) inches at all times.

4. Keep sidewalks free of clutter, including but not limited to: chalk drawings, handprints, memetic representations of any kind, sporting equipment, stray rubbish, unsightly leaves, liquids, or snow piles, toys, and any personal belongings not listed above.

5. No overnight guests.

6. All parks, gardens, pools, and other common areas close at sunset. Guards will be posted.

7. Tranquility hours strictly enforced after 10:00 p.m. and all day Sunday.

WINESAP

I was made for him.

It is morning, which is to say, it is the beginning of all things. It is bright and it is sharp and it is perfect and so is Sophia, who wakes alone to this singular thought, as she does every morning; to this honeyed, liquid thought and sunlight and sparrowsong and the softness of green shadows in a house that is far too big for her. Not that she complains—oh no, never, not Sophia, in whom the organ of dissatisfaction was somehow absent from birth. Her husband spoils her and she is grateful. But she never needed anything so grand! None of the other houses on their street are half as luxurious or imposing. And it is a long street, very long and very fine.

Sophia runs her hand over the place beside her where her husband so rarely sleeps these days and thinks it again, with as much joy:

I was made for him.

She moves in this echoing house like a flicker of a goldfish in the depthless trenches of the sea. Her long hair, bright and fine as cherry bark, snakes through a mountain of pillows. The dawn comes dancing in, as gold as you please, through vast crosshatched windows curtained in tapestries. Her bedside candle has burned down through the small hours to a thick, craggy nub. Her colorful blanket, still smooth and neat, for Sophia never has never had an anxious dream in all the deep violet nights of her life, streams away from her in all directions: a vast, peaceful province peopled by intricate embroidered roses, tatted lace peonies, quilted moonflowers, trailing ribbon-stitched clover, and the little cliffs and hollows of Sophia's rich body beneath the down.

Even the bed is so much bigger than she could ever need. Especially since she sleeps alone more nights than not. Her husband has important work and it never ends. Even when he is with her, he is always on call. Sophia does not mind. She has never minded. She keeps her own company very snugly and very well. There is something decadent in having this sea of silk and wool and wood all to herself. Sailing it into the unconquered country of her sleep like a pilgrim of the night. It feels like getting away with something, to have so much.

Getting out of bed is something of a mountaineering expedition. Her husband made her a little staircase down from the mattress to the floor so the delicate bones of her ankles never get jangled once. Sophia flexes her flat, golden-brown stomach and swings herself over the side, her smooth feet hitting the top stair with a satisfying sound, like a cup setting into its saucer.

She fetches her robe from a great brass hook in the wall. It is the color of earth before planting. It shines with quality. She knots the sash around her strong waist. It is too big for her. She drowns deliciously inside it. She does not need a robe. It is warm here and she has nothing to hide. But she enjoys the slippery kiss of it against her skin all the same.

Like everything else, it was a gift. From him to her. The world flows in that direction. Him to her. A river of forever.

She sits down at a huge vanity, so big she must pile up throw pillows on the seat just to see herself in the wide mirror, a polished oval glass ringed in carved wooden branches bearing figs and plums. Sophia has never been one for too much makeup. Scrubbed skin and hair is more than enough, her husband always says. But a little color in the cheek never hurt anyone. He never needs to know. If he thinks a woman wakes in the morning with shimmering eyes and a perfect pout, let him.

She ties her hair back with a white ribbon, stark as bare bone against her thick brown hair. Outside the windows, finches and starlings and lorikeets warm up for their daily concert in the park.

Sophia's long, clever fingers pull at the crystal knob on the vanity's top right-hand drawer. With a thrill of pleasure in this thing done each day for herself and herself alone, she takes out her little secret luxuries: a bronze compact with the puff tucked neatly inside, three slender brushes tipped with soft tufts of rabbit fur, and three small matching pots: clay for cold cream, silver for rouge, and gold for eyeliner. Kindly Mrs. Orpington tucked them into her grocery basket next to the sweet potatoes and the eggs and the new butter. Her neighbors are always looking out for her that way. Shy little treats, shy little smiles, shy little waves from down the road.

Sophia paints herself slowly, subtly, every sweep of the rabbit bristles against her skin as electric as a summer storm.

Today, as she does every day, Sophia will descend the grand staircase into the house. It takes some time. The teak steps rise so steep and tall she must perch on the lips of them like a child, stretching her legs down to brush the top of the next one, and only then scoot down safely, then repeat and repeat and repeat until her toes finally find the relief of the parquet floor. Her man carved each of the twenty-eight stairs round the edges with a million detailed leaves she must polish (plus the round silver moons that crown the banisters) once a week. But today is not polishing day! She needn't give one thought to the leaves and the moons.

No, today Sophia will clean the rest of the house. She imagines herself doing it before she begins, each task unfolding in her tidy mind as perfectly as a letter to herself.

She will sweep the floors with the heavy oak broom. Then she will scrub them with lemon water and good lavender soap she makes herself in their second guest bathroom so that the smell of lye will not trouble her mister. Only until the basement is finished! Then she will have room to spread out. Until then, Sophia is not allowed down into the cellar. It's dangerous, he tells her. So much old equipment lying around. She could get hurt.

Sophia doesn't ever want to get hurt. Or set one single soft foot where she is not allowed. What a thing to even imagine—just going right *into* a place he specifically told her wasn't safe! She excises this paradox from her thoughts and replaces it with a pleasant anticipation of how lovely the cellar will be when he finishes it, how convenient and enjoyable she will soon find it to make all her little treasures in a space built just for her.

After the floors, Sophia will beat the curtains and the rugs until the dust motes twinkle like stars in the thick warm air. She will collect all her husband's things from the sofas and the armchairs and the floor. It is laundry day, so she will wash all the linens and the bath towels and pin them up in the sun to dry from 11:00 a.m. to 1:00 p.m. exactly. Then, she will rinse the breakfast dishes, arrange flowers from the garden on the table where her husband will see them as soon as he comes home. *Orange roses for tonight,* she thinks. *Thorns carefully clipped off, of course.*

Plus white chrysanthemums and three bright fuchsia hibiscus branches. Yesterday was all lilies. Her sweetheart enjoys variety.

All this under her morning belt, she will eat a little spot of lunch, though a very little spot. He's warned her that heavy lunches make heavy hips, and Sophia wishes always to be his light. Afterward, she will clean her plate and cup until they shine, make herself presentable, and go about her errands on this very special day.

For today, Sophia has been invited next door to 3 Cedar Drive to see Mrs. Lyon, Mrs. Fische, and Mrs. Minke for tea. She's already wrapped up a little hostess gift for each of them. Sophia is the consummate guest, never a foot put wrong. Her husband laughs at the care she takes with such things. *Such a silly little head my Sophie has on her shoulders. Stop worrying so. They all love us. We're the life of the party. You don't have to bring presents every time to everybody. You don't have to bring any presents at all.*

But Sophia understands in the palest cells of marrow of her bones that everything she does, from the speed of her gait to the gifts she chooses to the sway of her hair as she walks down Cedar Drive, reflects upon him. And they *do* love him. It's so easy for him! The way Mrs. Crabbe tries to look busy to hide her blushing whenever he passes her in the garden on his way home from the office. The way Mr. Stagg fixes his hair and stands a little straighter when he ducks into their local for something cold and quiet. Sophia knows these are treasures that must be protected. She would never do the smallest thing that might risk how Mrs. Moray's dark eyes widen and her breath quickens when she glimpses the two of them strolling through the market of a Saturday. Heaven forbid. She would rather die.

He will never know how the gentle determination of her carefulness stokes and keeps the love of their neighbors. He does not need to. Sophia doesn't ask for praise or credit. *Is he the life of the party? Or is she?* Such questions! The party is alive, that's what matters. And whichever way one slices such a rich cake, her company is much in demand. Her social calendar overflows like a cup of wine. Everyone in Arcadia Gardens clamors to have her round. The honor of her presence at their home. The pleasure of her business at their establishment. The profound distress the absence of her witness would cause at this or that small ceremony of life.

Sophia strives to make certain they never have cause to regret her.

She pauses in her thoughts. She reaches out her long fingers to touch her image in the grand mirror. The glass is so cool beneath her skin.

After tea, she plans a stroll round the park, then to Mrs.

Lam's to pick up a bolt or two of the new turquoise wool in stock, a quick pop round the shops for supper supplies, then home to prepare it all before sunset, when it is not permitted to be roaming the streets.

It will be a lovely day. They are all lovely days. That's how lucky she is. That's how beautiful Sophia's life has always been and always will be. Not a minute unaccounted for. Not a season unsavored to the last dregs.

She is happy. Her husband is happy. The world is theirs.

I was made for him.

And then, for no reason whatsoever, no reason at all that she can think of later when she looks back and tries to explain everything that happened afterward and wishes so desperately that she'd never done it, so desperately that she almost faints away with the passion of longing to undo time and causality and uninvent the entire concept of furniture, Sophia looks down at the pull-knob on the top left-hand drawer of her vanity.

It isn't crystal, like the right-hand drawer. All the knobs on all the drawers are different. Copper, amber, white Bakelite, pewter. It makes a very pretty effect, like everything else her husband builds. The towering bed, the dizzying staircase, the splendid mirror, the high hook for her long robe, the heavy walnut table downstairs—as tall as a plowhorse at the shoulder, where she will later perch briefly, swinging her legs in the air, and eat honey and butter on toast points before heading out into the buttery, honeyed light of the afternoon.

Sophia stares at the top left-hand drawer as though she's never seen it before. It feels as though she hasn't. She never uses it, after all. Three pots and a compact hardly require all six drawers to fill. But this is *her* room. Her place at the mirror, boosted by all those pretty pillows. Every day of her married life, she's sat in this same place, tied her hair back with the same ribbon, and made herself into the same Sophia while the starlings sang. Every molecule of every object in this house is familiar to her.

So why does that drawer look so much like a filthy, ragged stranger standing suddenly in the corner of a brightly lit hall?

The pull-knob is stone. A rough, dull chunk of grey rock. She brushes it lightly with her fingertips. It is dusty. But Sophia allows nothing to gather dust. Not in this house. Not on her watch. Yet untold layers of dust particles float away into the shafts of sun like ash. Underneath, tiny ammonites press up out of the shale rock.

Sophia tells herself not to open it.

There is nothing inside, after all. She knows that! She knows the contents of every nook and cranny in this vast house. It's just an empty drawer. No reason whatsoever to waste her time on such a lump of nothing! Not when there is so much to do today! Such a silly little head she has on her shoulders. Doesn't he always say so?

And then Sophia pulls the stony knob anyway, because it *is* her house and her time to waste and she has every right to both.

The drawer is locked.

But nothing is locked in Arcadia Gardens. It's not that kind of neighborhood. They don't lock their front door at night. No one does. It's so unnecessary. They don't even have a key to this place—the real estate agent didn't mention one and after a while they just never bothered to have any made. They are safe here. That's the whole point. Nothing can touch them here.

Sophia picks up her silver brush and jimmies the thin handle into the crack between the countertop and the drawer.

It doesn't take much. Token resistance. The sound of the lock popping free is as satisfying as her shimmying, stretching foot finding purchase on the first step of the staircase.

Sophia blinks slowly and stares into the drawer.

It is not empty.

There's a hairbrush in there. A hairbrush she has never seen before. And beside it, a lock of hair.

The brush is enormous. The back is made of antler or bone, the bristles no soft spring rabbit, but hard, sharp, wild boar. She picks it up and turns it over and over in her hands. The size of the thing makes her feel like a child juggling some forbidden adult prize she can barely hold on to. Someone has burned runes and designs and symbols Sophia cannot understand, except to think they are beautiful in a brutal sort of way, all over the handle and body of the thing: dark, angular, slashing. Maybe they're letters. Maybe they're stallions' heads. Maybe they're something very, very else.

But it is the lock of hair that troubles her more.

It is not her hair.

Sophia's hair is soft and fine and curly and the color of good, sweet roasting pecans. The hair in the drawer is straight, coarse, and black as a secret. Each strand is so thick you could almost write with it. No one they know has hair like that. Not Mrs. Crabbe or Mrs. Lam or Mrs. Lyon or even beautiful Mrs. Palfrey two blocks over on Olive Street.

Like a horse's mane.

Perhaps it *is* a horse's mane.

But why would anyone tie the hair of a horse so lovingly, with a white ribbon just the same as the one Sophia uses to pull her hair away from her graceful collarbones every morning?

She puts it to her nose and smells the hair. The stench of it floods her brain and makes her gag: spices and rotting flesh and sour, private sweat and hot sands stretching away into a burning, lonely nothingness.

Slowly, as if underwater, as if someone else has been given run of her limbs, Sophia unties her own hair and begins to comb it with the great bone brush.

Tears float into the crescents of her eyes, and she does not know why.

IDARED

8. The front and back yards are to be used for leisure and ornamentation only. Flowers and hedges are acceptable if well-maintained and not allowed to obstruct sight lines into the interior of the property in order to ensure that all activity remains clearly visible from outside the home. No vegetable plantings or other agricultural activity is permitted.

9. It is forbidden to construct outbuildings for the purposes of industry such as beekeeping, the milling of grain or the tanning of hides, beermaking, soapmaking, cheese-making, pottery, weaving, small vehicle repair, dancing, or other.

EMPIRE

Mrs. Lyon lounges grandly on her long green sofa. Her broad, powerful hips press into the plush as she stirs her tea with deliberate slowness. Mrs. Fische has flopped casually onto the floor, her silver hair floating free of any attempt to confine it, relishing her fourth cup. Mrs. Minke perches nervously on an embroidered stool, tapping her teaspoon against the saucer in a quick, staccato rhythm like an over-wound clock. The three hostess gifts lie unopened before them on Mrs. Lyon's yellow wicker coffee table.

"I'm sure I've no idea what you mean," Mrs. Lyon says silkily. She yawns, her pink tongue showing in her pretty mouth. Sophia blushes at such an intimate sight.

"A hairbrush, you say?" bubbles Mrs. Fische. "Nothing so odd about that."

Mrs. Minke sets her teaspoon down and picks it up again. Her sleek brown hair perfectly frames her small, pert face. "You must have so many hairbrushes, Sophie, darling," she chirps brightly. "With that great slap of a man of yours spoiling you so! That's all it is. You've got so many luxurious things you can't keep track of them all! We should all have such problems!"

Sophia frowns doubtfully.

"The simplest explanation, really," Mrs. Fische reassures her, and reaches for the teapot for a fifth cup.

"Slow down, you guppy, you'll slurp me out of house and home. I shall have to make another pot already." Mrs. Lyon takes her teapot to the kitchen to put another kettle on.

"It's so delicious, I can hardly help myself," Mrs. Fische burbles happily. "It's not my fault you make the Lord's own pot! Mrs. Bea's blend, if I'm not mistaken?"

"Indeed." Mrs. Lyon nods with pleasure as she returns with a fresh, gleaming tray. It is so nice to have nice things, after all. "A new recipe, just harvested from the community gardens. Something with apple blossoms, I think, I wasn't really listening. You know how Mrs. Bea will go on if you let her."

The sunlight turns the china to fire as Mrs. Lyon pours. The pattern glows incandescent—slim gazelles and fat sheep prancing through interlocking curls of long, braided grass.

"But the lock of hair, you see," Sophia protests weakly.

She hates to contradict anyone. Especially since she is quite a ways younger than her teatime companions, especially Mrs. Fische. They know so much more than she does, about so many things. Silver hair, Mrs. F always says, is the medal won by wisdom. Sophia touches her curls self-consciously and wonders if she will get any silver of her own. She doubts it is possible. Not for such a silly little head and a silly little heart.

"I'm not at all sure what you're trying to say, dear," snaps Mrs. Minke irritably. Her dark eyes appraise Sophia up and down. "Do you think he's been . . . *disloyal* to you? Is that it?"

"I don't know!" Sophia says helplessly. She knows she oughtn't. What will this do to the widening of Mrs. Moray's eyes? But she's so afraid. It dribbles out of her like blood. "Yesterday I could never imagine it. But today? And I can't help but think he's away so often with work . . . how am I to know what goes on when we're apart?"

"But with *who,* darling?" Mrs. Fische tuts, looming greedily over the new pot of tea. "Old Mrs. Elke and Mrs. Hounde down at the farmer's market? With *those* waistlines?" The other ladies laugh indulgently. "Perhaps Mrs. Hart, with her spots and nervous disposition? Or Mrs. Marten and her irresistible furry upper lip?" A reluctant smile begins to pull at Sophia's rosy lips. In the friendly air of Mrs. Lyon's sitting room, it really does seem so foolish.

"One of *us?*" Mrs. Minke squeals. "You don't think your beau is gallivanting around with one of *us,* do you? Oh, you couldn't. Just try to imagine it! Pawing at Mrs. L! Flip-flapping against old Mrs. F? Rolling around in the grass with *me*? You

can't. It's too ridiculous! Who could compare with you, Sophie? You're so perfectly lovely and perfectly good and perfectly sweet as a perfect orange. Everyone knows it. Don't get
your soft little neck twisted. As far as that man can see, you're
the only woman in the world."

"As far as *anyone* can see. I've caught Mr. Lyon stealing
a glance or three, I don't mind telling you." Mrs. Lyon rolls
her eyes and tosses her thick, dark golden hair gaily.

"Oh, nonsense!" Sophia cries out, her face burning red.

"It's true! Oh, pish-posh, it's no shadow on my grass. He
wouldn't dare. I'd eat his head! But he gets such a *hollow*
look in his big lazy eyes when he sees you coming up the
walk without your fat slice of man at your side. I know that
look. We all know it. The look of the hunt. Oh, I remember
when he looked at me that way!"

"But your sweetie still looks at you as hungry as ever,"
Mrs. Minke reassures her, patting her hand. "I've seen it
with my own eyes. One quiver of your lip and he's fit to
hunt you and only you to the ends of time and back."

The girls giggle and Sophia does feel better. She *has* been
silly, really. Her husband works with all manner of animals,
after all. It's probably a snipping off some prize mare he
forgot to tell her about. Far too coarse and thick and wild-
smelling for a woman. A woman *couldn't* smell like that.
Sophia doesn't smell like that. What was she thinking? It
all seems so insignificant, now, in Mrs. Lyon's sitting room,

surrounded by bright lamps and good china and the laughter of good ladies.

Who, indeed?

A quiet, polite knock at the door cracks open the afternoon like a spoon tapping an egg.

"Oh!" Mrs. Lyon exclaims, clapping her big hands together. Her round butterscotch eyes shine. "We have company! Clear the tea things, Mrs. Minke, there's a good girl. The Maestro doesn't partake, you know."

"You never mentioned company," Sophia whispers.

Her shoulders tense. Anxiety simmers back through her veins in a sour flood. Sophia does not like to be surprised. It hardly ever happens to her. Perhaps once, when she first saw the enormous house on Cedar Drive. Possibly twice. When she met her husband for the first time, the size and the color of him, the hum of his voice, how completely her bones and her sinew and the musculature of her heart knew they belonged to him. Nothing was ever the same again after. Surprises did that to you. Nasty things. Lying in wait. A surprise, even a little one, means a change in the world, and Sophia likes her world as it is. She likes it so much.

But Mrs. Lyon does not agree. She smiles with feline smugness. "Why would I? It's a surprise! Now go on and answer the door, Sophie, it's not polite to keep a man waiting on the stoop."

Sophia places her slender hand on the latch. She studies the little dapple of shadow and light over her fingers, a flutter of red like blood projected there through the high roses outside Mrs. Lyon's front window. The wind comes. The red breaks apart. It is only her hand again. She opens the door and looks up into a stranger's face.

He is tall, taller than her husband even, but so skinny, a riot of golden hair tangling up from his skull like a crown of buttercups. His eyes burn into her, staring, staring, looking for something he cannot find in the very cellar of her being. Oh, she hates them! She hates his eyes instantly and forever. They are blue and green and brown all at once, fringed with long lashes, so bright Sophia looks away. An ungovernable shyness cripples her. She does not want to look at the stranger. His gaze peels her open like an unripe green almond. He should not look at her like that. Sophia does not want to look at any man but her husband. She does not want any strangers in her life at all. She crosses her arms over her chest to keep him out. He frowns at this gesture, as though it is not entirely his fault.

"Mr. Semengelof, come in!" purrs Mrs. Lyon. "Mrs. Minke, Mrs. Fische, this is Mr. Semengelof, he is a most *extraordinary* musician, just back from travels abroad—you *will* tell us all about your journeys through all those thrilling foreign climes, won't you?"

"If you wish." He bows slightly at the waist. His voice

isn't like the voices of the women. Sophia hardly thinks she hears him at all. She *feels* his voice, sawing over her heart like an unresined bow.

"Where did you go?" Sophia says softly. What a strange name. What a strange man. She wishes he would just turn around and leave again, immediately.

But he does not. Mr. Semengelof turns to fix her with that every-colored stare again. He does not say one single merciful word for a long time. Far too long for any sort of manners.

"Far," he answers, as though that suffices.

Sophia wants to scream. She can feel the scream trying to claw up out of her belly.

"Well, I'm sure I can't imagine anywhere better than our own Arcadia Gardens!" Mrs. Lyon sniffs.

Mrs. Minke's small eyes narrow even further with gossipy delight. "He was tracking a *criminal*, Sophia. Can you imagine? A criminal, just outside our gates! It's positively *thrilling*. She could have descended upon any one of us, at any moment! Snatched our babies in the night or ransacked our homes! Oh! Too horrid! It makes one feel just terrifically *alive*."

Sophia can hear the scream in her head, echoing off the walls of her skull. She tries to speak normally. Is she speaking normally? Is her voice too loud in this suddenly small room?

"What did she do? The criminal, I mean."

Mr. Semengelof's jaw moves beneath his skin. He seems to see no one but her.

"She broke the contract," he says evenly. "The Association's terms are very clearly enumerated in the Agreement. She had no excuse." He pauses. His eyes crawl all over her, pressing for a way in. "I do hope others will not be so careless."

Sophia knows she should stop talking. The longer she talks, the longer this man will stay. She doesn't mean to open her mouth at all. Her words just seem to *happen* to her.

"Are you a policeman?" she almost whispers. *Be quiet, Sophia!*

Mr. Semengelof turns his head to one side curiously. Then he keeps turning it—slowly, slowly—further, further—sickeningly far, until his neck must surely break, but does not. And then further still. Sophia glimpses the back of his skull for a moment before his gaze comes back round the other side to throttle her again, like a terrible owl. Mrs. Minke and Mrs. Fische keep smiling eagerly, as though nothing untoward has happened. Sophia's jaws throb with the effort of keeping that scream on the right side of her teeth.

"After a fashion," Mr. Semengelof says at last. "You might call me that. Among other names." But the peculiar way he says *you* makes Sophia quite certain he means her alone.

Mrs. F and Mrs. L and Mrs. M might call him by his other names. But for Sophia and for her alone, he has claimed his title.

Mrs. Lyon hurries on past such unpleasant talk. "In *any* event, Mr. Semengelof has come to stay with us awhile and tutor my little ones in the musical arts. Impossible wee things, not a spot of talent between them, but what can you do? No matter, he'll have them choiring to the heavens in no time, won't you, Maestro?"

The maestro finally ducks under the doorframe and stands awkwardly in the sitting room. His body seems to take up more space than all the four of them put together. But his movements are so graceful and delicate Sophia feels tears needling the backs of her eyes. Tears, not at his twisting neck, but at the utterly usual movements of this strange man with his strange name. Tears, because the act of sitting on the sofa, when performed by Mr. Semengelof, is more beautiful than roses. Her husband does not move like that. He *thuds* when he walks. He *thuds* when he sits. He *thuds* when he eats and when he drinks and even when he sleeps. Sophia likes his thudding, she always has. When he *thuds,* the world listens and gets out of his way. That is her whole understanding of men.

Sophia does not think Mr. Semengelof even knows how to *thud.* He almost seems as though he could fly.

"At your service, Mrs. Lyon. Good afternoon, Mrs. Minke,

Mrs. Fische." The music teacher inclines his head. "Hello, Sophia," he says. Her tears spill finally down her face. "It's an honor to meet you."

"Me?" Sophia whispers. Her throat's gone so dry. She longs for Mrs. Lyon's tea back again.

"Yes," the stranger says, and the other ladies sigh with excitement. "A very great honor. I think we shall be seeing much of each other, now that we are to be neighbors. For a time."

"Oh, I doubt it. I'm such a bore, really." Sophia blushes and waves her hand. "I'm certainly not anything to be honored about." She does not like to blush; it makes her feel exposed. She hates her face for doing it to her.

"Won't you give us a little recital, Mr. S?" Mrs. Lyon purrs, coaxing. "There is nothing better in the afternoon than a meal and a bit of music."

The music teacher glides across the living room to a piano with a framed picture of Mr. Lyon on its lid. He sits at the bench and settles his extraordinarily long fingers on the keys, yellowed as old teeth. His back looms long and dark. But something about it almost glows. Something lovely against his shoulder blades Sophia cannot quite see, even as she stares into his spine.

Without looking round, he says, with a gentleness like a feather falling:

"Are you happy, Sophia?"

She blinks. She forgets instantly the scream shoving at her bones.

Is she *happy*?

She doesn't understand. She has never considered it. It is possible to be so entirely happy you never ask the question. She is a full glass submerged in water. Neither nor both full and empty. The inquiry, though kind, has no meaning for her.

"Oh, certainly she is, Mr. Semengelof!" Mrs. Fische interrupts quickly, her voice floating up through the stuffy parlor air. "Terribly so!"

"Of course she's happy," Mrs. Minke snaps, dropping her spoon onto her saucer with finality.

"We're *all* happy, Maestro," Mrs. Lyon pronounces brightly, but Sophia watches her dig her long nails like claws deep into the pale yellow arm of her sofa. "Positively blissful. Don't you worry about us."

Sophia says nothing. They have answered for her. She does not need to speak. It is always a blessing and a relief to be spoken for. But they all stare at her, waiting, until the quiet mounts to such a roar that she can hear time crawl.

"I *am* happy, Mr. Semengelof. How could I be otherwise? I am fed, I am housed, I am busy, I am loved."

Her voice catches on the last word. She thinks of the bone hairbrush. The stiff, stinking pig bristles. The black marks. The shaft of reeking hair.

She falls back on the familiar. She wraps herself in its comfort.

"I was made for him," she finishes, the quaver in her voice infinitesimally small.

"Do you lack for anything, Sophia? Or perhaps instead there is some small displeasing item in whose removal you would rejoice?"

Sophia could tell him now. About the brush and the hair and the smell and the dust on the ammonites in the stone knob on her dressing table drawer. It almost seems as though he already knows, that he's given her this and only this chance to have it all done with.

She does not know why she lies. She only knows she cannot tell the truth. They are *hers*. Her house. Her dressing table. Her ammonites. Her hideous boar-brush. Her secrets to keep.

"No," Sophia says smoothly. "Nothing."

The music teacher sighs, a long exhale of sadness. But he seems satisfied. He begins to play, and for a moment Sophia fully and truly thinks she will die. The sound of it is a knife, if a knife could kiss, and the kiss could turn the color of morning. There is no sense to the song. It crashes and whispers and cajoles and weeps and admonishes and commands all at once, without progression from one feeling to the next. Yet it contains a perfection that is twin to pain.

Sophia does not die. The kiss and the knife and the color

go on and on. The man does not play music. The man *is* music.

As the song like pure starlight fills the room, Sophia slowly draws up her knees to her chest, wraps her arms around her whole self, and begins to rock back and forth. The three older women idly open their hostess gifts, un-affected and unconcerned. They exclaim silently over them, showing them off as the music teacher's slender dark back bends over his work.

A knob of fresh cheese Sophia made herself, a squirming mass of tiny pink bloodworm larvae, and a sopping wet red lump of fresh, glistening meat: a heart, still bright with oxygenation, just this side of beating.

Mrs. Fische plucks up a helping of larvae and drops it into her mouth, sucking her fingers with relish. Mrs. Minke sinks her sharp teeth into the cheese. Mrs. Lyon licks greedily at the severed aorta of the heart.

Sophia smiles at them. Seeing their pleasure pushes the music and the strange man and the scream far down into the root system of her mind. The tension pops like a moon-flower opening. Ease slides down her limbs.

She *is* happy, after all.

Sophia's smile unfurls as pure and perfect as the first smile ever managed. They like her gifts. They like *her*. She is appreciated. She is loved. It is such a wonderful thing in this world, to have friends.

SNOWSWEET

10. Holiday displays and other celebrations are prohibited. Every day in Arcadia is pleasurable and special. Holidays are therefore superfluous.

11. It is forbidden in the strictest terms to give the passcode for the exterior Arcadia Gardens gate to anyone not a signatory to or in current violation of this Agreement. Transgression will result in immediate eviction.

12. Suffering of any kind is and shall be considered contraband.

13. No children shall be tolerated on or around the Property. This Agreement covers two (2) Residents only, from signing until termination by the Association. Any conception, whether brought to term or otherwise, shall void this contract in its entirety.

KEEPSAKE

The sun wriggles down between the green foothills that ring Arcadia Gardens like a wedding band. Time passes without pressing its claim. Oranges ripen on the tree, passion fruit on the vine, the wool on the backs of hand-raised, heirloom-breed communal sheep lengthens by the barest fraction of a centimeter, and Sophia sits down, alone at a laden table. She watches the golden juice glisten on the breast of a roast chicken and roll down the rich mound of meat to pool on the clean china plate beneath.

Her husband does not come home that night. Sophia accepts this as she accepts the presence of gravity. As she accepts everything else. His work often takes him far afield and into the next day. A freelancer knows not the meaning of the words *day shift* or *night shift*! Perhaps Mrs. Lyon or Mrs. Minke know how to dislike their lives and scold their husbands. Sophia has never had the knack.

Once it is full dark outside, she lights the candles and eats her share alone. She swings her legs back and forth under the chair like a small girl. She will leave the larger portion for him, of course. It takes so little to fill her up. Sophia admires her table setting, its symmetry and balance. Roast chicken stuffed with pears and citron, buttered peas with mint and thyme, fresh bread rich and yellow with extra eggs, salted cucumbers, and a fig-and-date trifle lavished in pink pomegranate cream. Sophia savors each bite mindfully, aware of its source and its aim, grateful for its weight in her belly, its benefit to her body.

She has not thought of Mr. Semengelof for hours, since before she began dressing the roast. Honest work banishes bad memories with such efficiency!

Sometimes, on these nights she spends alone, Sophia looks at her bountiful table and can almost see that something should be there that isn't. Not her husband or her friends, but others, others she cannot quite name or even imagine, shadows, phantoms of a future unlike the present, *somethings* to fill these eight chairs round the dining set. That has always seemed strange to her. Eight chairs, when it's always been just the two of them.

Sophia shakes her head. What has gotten into her today? She will ask Mrs. Lyon's little ones to supper on the weekend, and they will need the chairs then. Goodness! How many times has she hosted their neighbors? That's all the chairs have ever been or ever will be for. What else? Who else?

How quickly the blue-green of twilight brings wildness to the mind.

To tame herself, she recalls Mr. Orpington's shop that afternoon. The sign above the door, painstakingly lettered in gold: *Orpington's Organic Co-Op: Your Needs Are Our Wants.* And just outside the door, in the same pretty penmanship, that long, lovely poster announcing the summer show:

Tomorrow at the Arcadia Gardens
Municipal Amphitheater:
An Evening of Earthly Delights!
A Pantomime: Memories of Bliss to Come
To Be Followed by Ice Cream and Dancing
Presented by Your Gracious Hosts
Mrs. Palfrey, Mrs. Moray, and Mrs. Wolfe!

She remembers with pleasure selecting the peas from the barrel like emeralds, sliding the silver scoop down into the infinite depths of little green gems and up again. Smelling the heavy red pomegranates with all those garnet crystal seeds inside. The basket of brown and blue eggs offered to her by young Mrs. Orpington, her eyes shining with strange tears, her beautiful black curls tumbling down her back, bashful and proud to have so much to give her favorite customer. The russet hen that scampered across the shop floor and leapt up toward Sophia with a crow of joy, the very bird that rested now on the good china plate before her. How she caught the bird and it snuggled into her arms, looking up at her with expectant adoration.

"She is yours, sweet girl," Mr. Orpington said with moist, dark eyes. "Enjoy her."

"Are you happy, Sophia?" asked Mrs. Orpington hopefully, still clutching her basket of eggs.

"Why does everyone keep asking me that?" Sophia replied. She laughed, because it seemed the right sort of thing to do, but they did not laugh back.

"It is important," answered Mr. Orpington quietly.

Sophia frowned, and at the sight of her frown, Mrs. Orpington began to tremble.

"Are you?" Sophia said, and as she remembers it, she suspects she might not have sounded very nice about it, even though she *felt* nice toward the old dears. "Happy, I mean."

"Of course," the shopkeeper whispered hoarsely, his eyes fixed on the clucking bird she cradled in the angle of her elbow. "Of course we are."

Sophia hurried away, clutching their pretty red hen and their emerald peas and their sugar-clotted dates and figs and their blue eggs and their clay jar of cream she could bring back or not any time it was convenient for her and their trembling and their words in her arms.

She should have answered politely, she knows better, and she curses her own manners. She will go back tomorrow and apologize. After all, she *is* happy. What is so hard about saying so, and to those who have never done her any harm? What if this makes them surly toward her husband when he comes to buy his coffee and his bacon? She could not bear that.

She is happy. Sophia is happy. Why could she not tell them?

⹈⹈⹈

She clears away the detritus of supper in silence. For a moment, she wishes Mr. Semengelof was there to play his piano and fill her head with something other than herself. But she remembers the actuality of Mr. Semengelof and retracts her wish as quickly as a cat's claws.

Sophia flows into the rituals of the kitchen. She steps up and down from the stepstool her husband made her as she gives each object over to its proper home. Plates in the great cabinet. Glasses in the china case. Pans to soak in the sink. Bones in the silver pot on the stove to render into broth for tomorrow's soup, liquid golden fat in a jar in the icebox for tomorrow's frying. Nothing wasted. Nothing left out. Flatware in the drawer, knives washed and laid out to dry, ready to be slotted neatly back into the wooden knife block. Sophia slides the biggest blade into the biggest slot.

But it does not fit. It catches on something. The blade will not go. It makes a sound when it finds its obstruction. A scratching and a clunking. Sophia sets the long carving knife down on the counter and tips the knife block over, patting the bottom like a bottle of oil to get the dregs out. The obstruction tumbles into her hand.

It is a bone.

Brown and dry and old and small. It has not known meat or juice for years. *It must be a bit of chicken bone. I overlooked it stuck to the knife and shoved it in,* she chides herself. *Lazy. Slovenly.* But her heart beats fast and her stomach floods itself with acid and she knows, she *knows* she had nothing to do with this. He carves the roast, not her. It's too big for her little hands, he always laughs, babying the blade with an oilcloth before putting it away himself.

There are marks on the bone, the same marks that slashed up the back of the hairbrush, black scaldings, black letters in a language set in direct opposition to the friendly kinds of letters that spell out *Orpington's Organic Co-Op* over the place where the evening roast flies joyfully to your arms.

And it is not a chicken bone. Sophia wants it to be. More than anything, in this blue-washed moment with the stars craning their necks toward her in particular, more than anything she wants it to be a chicken bone. To smell of sage and rosemary and butter. But it doesn't, because it can't. It smells only of time and loneliness and wild, hot, endless sands.

Sophia cannot help knowing what she knows. She is standing in her beautiful open floor-plan kitchen in her perfect sprawling house holding the tip of a human finger.

CORTLAND

14. Smoking of any substance and drinking of spirits by female Residents are not permitted due to possible damages incurred to the Property.

15. If approached by the Association's Representatives, Residents will behave with decorum and deference, providing any documents, evidence, testimony, or information requested, and executing with promptness any and all solicited action(s).

CAMEO

The moon melts in through the big bay windows of 1 Cedar Drive like cold butter over hot bread. Nightingales and whip-poor-wills and kingfishers tune up their throats as a gentle mist lifts from the street into the summer night.

Sophia wakes. She fell asleep on the couch, too afraid to go up to that massive bed where the shadows looked like long fingers reaching for her in the moonlight. She looks down across the landscape of her drowsy body and sees that a tiny grey field mouse has curled up in the arch of her naked foot. Its round ears twitch with dreams of clover and owls.

Sophia stares. She does not leap away. It has the right to sleep in what shelter it can find, poor thing.

"Go on," she whispers, and moves her toes ever so little.

The field mouse opens its black eyes. It does not leap either. It watches her. It leans warmly, possessively against her foot. It opens its mouth.

A shadow falls across Sophia's belly in the shape of a

curved knife. She looks up unbreathing and she is not alone, not even so alone as a woman with a mouse. A heron stands outside her window, a waterbird as tall as a man, its fish-shredding beak pointed at her heart, the blue of its feathers glowing like wet ink in the first drops of sunlight. It taps the glass with its beak. Harder, harder, until it is not a tapping but a stabbing. A spiderweb of broken glass pops open. The heron opens its mouth. A long hiss rises up from its gullet.

Give it to me, rasps the heron. It is impossible, impossible, and yet the eyes of the creature are the every-colored eyes of Mr. Semengelof. It speaks with the voice of the music teacher. Pure song. Pure pity. *Give it to me and I will take it away forever.*

Sophia's muscles thicken with the rigor of horror. She cannot move. She cannot get away. She cannot understand. She tries to obey, but she is so afraid.

Give it to me and I will take it not only from your house but from your mind. It will not trouble you again. You will not even remember that it troubled you at all.

The field mouse blinks its beautiful eyes. *It's okay,* it whispers. *It's best this way. You don't deserve it.*

The bird stops. It jerks its sleek head toward the door and flies away in one long fluid unfurling of wing and intent. Enough. *But it has shown it can get to me,* Sophia thinks. *It can get to me whenever it wants.*

The mouse has fled just the same.

Her husband enters the house without knocking, as he always does. Drops his things on the foyer floor without a care.

"I am home! I am here! Where is my wife?"

Sophia is on her feet and in his arms in the same fluid unfurling movement as the heron's ascent. It is him, it is him, and there can be nothing wrong now, how stupid she's been, how young and small and reckless with herself. Her husband holds her so tight. His arms dwarf her, envelop her, the most exquisite suffocation. He smells of growing greens and blackberries and ripe hops and deep, tilled, tended earth. And a little of blood and milk and musk, always, yes, of the animals he works with, their bodies and their breath and their hot, quick life. No smell excites Sophia more than this.

"My love, my love," she whispers.

His big hand cups her head, strokes her long hair, and then he wants her, of course he does, and she wants him too, his kisses and his strength and his warmth and his need.

Your Needs Are Our Wants.

"Are you happy, Sophia?" he whispers urgently as he devours her.

He says her name over and over, until it no longer sounds like her name at all, but someone else's, and for a moment,

Sophia could swear it *is* someone else's name. Other vowels and other consonants, strangers in the halls of her ears. But she shakes her head against his chest and the moment floats away. The world is Sophia again. *Sophia, Sophia, Sophia.* The tickle of his breath in the curve of her neck; the tickle of the field mouse's fur on the curve of her foot; the tickle of the glass breaking beneath the heron's beak.

"You are happy, aren't you? Aren't you?"

"Yes, my darling," Sophia sighs, and she is not lying. Not yet. The mingling of their breath is a biome in which only the truth can thrive. "Yes."

She serves him an early breakfast in the easing dark, as light on her feet as dancing. All sins forgotten in the slicing of toast, all foolishness in the hot, real grounded smell of good cheese, and won't they have a day, the two of them, strolling the parks, checking on their squash blossoms and snap peas and olives in the Community Garden, carefully helping the pollen along with paintbrushes if need be, poor lazy squashes. And then they'll go to the show. Mrs. Palfrey and Mrs. Moray and Mrs. Wolfe's summer spectacular! How considerate of him to come home in time. Sophia will sit in the amphitheater as a cool silvery evening breeze relieves the heat and the fireflies begin to click on in the trees, snuggled into the safety of him, treasured as gold, waiting for the lights to go down and the music to start.

I was made for him, she thinks, *and that is all that matters.*

Sophia reaches for the little paring knife to slice off last night's still-moist chicken to crosshatch over the toast. Her hand stops all on its own. It hovers.

Yes, there is a show tonight, and ice cream and dancing and a million fireflies like wishes, but there is also a bone in the knife block. There is a bone in the knife block because Sophia put it back where she found it, not knowing what else to do. There is a bone in the knife block and someone's hair in the upstairs drawer. The egg yolks wriggle wetly on the half-prepared plate. She will not ask him. She will not. She trusts him. She is happy. Sophia is happy.

He roars for his breakfast and she hurries. Sticks the carving knife back in where it will not fit because someone's fingertip is in there, leaves the blade jutting halfway out, trembling slightly in its slot even after she's gone.

Sophia watches her man eat. His appetite is as enormous as their bed, their table, their chairs, their candlesticks. It gratifies her deepest being. She would rather watch him eat than eat herself, in perfect honesty.

"Your work has gone well, my love?" she asks warmly.

"Very well! It always does. It is hard going but I never give up. My supervisor is very pleased with me. I may even get a bonus soon."

"Oh, how wonderful!" Sophia exclaims, and claps her hands.

"Yes, it is," he agrees between mouthfuls of chicken and toast.

She kisses his forehead. "*You* are wonderful," she whispers.

"Yes, I am!" he laughs. "But you're only buttering me up like an ear of corn because you want to go to the pantomime tonight."

Sophia frowns. Her brow furrows. She does not understand.

"No, I'm not. You *are* wonderful. You are my whole heart."

"Yes, yes." He rolls his eyes. "But you do want to go to the amphitheater, don't you? See all your friends, dance and applaud and all that sort of nonsense?"

"Well, of course I do, but . . ." Sophia struggles to comprehend what he can mean. She believed in his wonder, so she said it to him. How could such a thing have purpose other than itself?

"I knew it!" her husband crows triumphantly. Sophia's chest feels tight. Her shoulders tense against her spine, little spasms of dissonance.

"You think it's nonsense?" she says quietly.

"Only because it *is* nonsense. That stuff's all for you, darling. Dancing, theater, music, fraternization—women's work! Me, I'd be happy sleeping out on the ground among the herds, eating what falls off the vine, never seeing another soul. Other than you, of course!" Sophia casts her eyes down. "Oh, don't look so stricken! I like that you like it! Keeps me civilized. We'll go, I promise. You watch the show, I'll watch you. And we'll both be happy."

Sophia does not look up. She will not ask him. She will not. She will not.

"My love," she says into her chest.

Her husband wipes the crumbs and grease of his breakfast off on his knees. "What is it now? I've already said we'll go."

"My love, when we are apart, what do you do?"

His great bright eyes narrow. "What are you talking about? I work. I work hard. I do it for *us,* Soph."

"I know! I know, beloved. But what I mean is . . . what *else* do you do? Do you have friends, outside Arcadia?"

"My supervisors, if that's what you're on about."

"No, I thought, perhaps . . . new people. New women?" Women with long, coarse, dark, wild hair. Women missing a fingertip . . .

He laughs. Sophia adores his laugh. When her dearheart laughs, nothing dark can stay. "Is *that* what you've got your little heart in a knot over?" He grabs her in his arms and swings her around as easily as a clean sheet. He is so big and she is so small. He can make her fly. "Not possible. You are the only woman in the world, Sophia," he says, pressing his cheek to hers. "You were made for me."

He sets her down and Sophia gasps, breathless, weeping. Relief. Relief to be wrong and to be his.

"Is that dissatisfaction I see?" her husband asks, lifting her chin with his thumb. His eyes search hers. "It couldn't be, not my Sophie."

"No," she gasps. "Never. I love you. I'm such a silly thing, you know. Such a silly thing."

He looks over her head. His face shifts, darkens, pales, like clouds moving on water. "What happened to the window?"

"I have no idea," Sophia says, and immediately recoils from herself. She cannot understand why she lied, and for the second time in a day. Only that she has, and she cannot take either of them back, and the world is changed because of it.

GINGER GOLD

16. At no time and for no reason will the Residents be permitted to transfer ownership of the Property, sublet, subdivide, sell, or otherwise abandon it. Dissolution of this Agreement may occur only at the discretion of the Association.

17. No fences or other obstructions for the purpose of partitioning Arcadia Gardens properties are permitted. Be a good neighbor and you will have good neighbors!

18. Roof shingles are to conform and be no larger than three inches by three (3x3) inches, in shades of Gevurah Grey or Binah Brown.

19. Fraternization and assembly may occur only in private residences or in the following designated public areas: the Community Garden, within six (6) feet of all shops and business fronts, Chikidel Community Pool, Dilmun Park and Promenade, the Hesperides Riverwalk, and the Arcadia Gardens Municipal Amphitheater. Loitering, dallying, idling, lingering, or malingering on streets, sidewalks, and other non-designated locations is forbidden.

GALA

The night dazzles Sophia.

Fireflies blaze in the brush just as she thought they might. The amphitheater benches fill slowly with all the friendly faces of her dear and darling neighborhood. Everyone buzzes with the thrill of being allowed out of doors at night, granted dispensation for a special event.

There flits Mrs. Bea up and down the stands with her covered mugs of tea for sale. There sits Mr. Breame with his big belly and his lady and all their little ones bubbling around them. There lounges Mrs. Baer with her big heavy coat, even in summer, fishing raspberries out of the greasepaper bag she got from Mrs. Elke, the broad, pretty brunette who rules the farmer's market every weekend like a kingdom.

And yes, there goes Mrs. Lyon!

And all her little ones, and Mrs. Minke and Mrs. Fische besides, waving to her, to Sophia, the luckiest woman the earth could imagine. And there is Mr. Semengelof too. He sits straight-backed as a heron in the lower rows, the last of the sun a corona ringing his hair. He lifts a solemn hand to them in greeting. Sophia looks away quickly. Her husband grins and waves to the music teacher as though they are old friends.

"Do you know him?" Sophia asks, and then feels foolish. Of course he does. He knows everyone.

"We work together," he says, drinking from his bottle. His tan throat moves gorgeously as he swallows.

Sophia blinks. He has never mentioned a music teacher, nor can he carry a tune. So it must be Semengelof's other work that her husband knows. "Did you help him find that criminal?" she whispers. "Is that what you do when you don't come home? Hunt?"

His head whips round toward her. He lowers his voice to a half-growl and engulfs her upper arm in his inexorable hand. "Who told you about her?" he asks urgently. "Who?"

"No one," she insists. She tries to get free of his grip, but she is only small compared to him. "No one, it was only a bit of gossip."

He storms off toward Semengelof. His handprint flushes pink and harsh on her skin. The two men speak urgently, but Sophia cannot hear; too many other voices swarm up toward her, a protective wall against whatever is happening down there in the front rows.

"Come on, kittens," Mrs. Lyon chortles loudly, and shuffles her brood toward Sophia, trailing the other ladies behind her like an ellipsis. "Where's your better half, my dear?" she asks, stretching languidly and plopping herself down on the rough-hewn stone slab beside her friend.

And he appears again at her back, arms full, as though he only left to get treats.

"Right here, Mrs. Lyon," booms the voice of Sophia's beloved, her devotion, who could never hurt anyone, not really, not ever. She understands that so completely now, seeing him in the firefly-light, among the throng of their little village where they both belong, the color high and happy in his cheeks, his hair combed until it shone, just for her, just for her to love a little better than if it were tangled. He hands her a slab of honeycomb wrapped in Mrs. Orpington's greasepaper and keeps a bottle of sweet, cold wine from the Guernseys' vineyard for himself. "The life of the party, reporting for duty!"

He loves her. He will love her until the end of always. The bone and the hair are nothing in the face of all that he's given her. A bit of sheep's foot that didn't make it into the stockpot. A scrap of horsehair to make into rope. Or perhaps it was a test, to see if she would doubt him. Yes, yes, that had to be the answer. A test. And Sophia would never fail.

But in her mind she sees the spiderweb of broken glass irising out from the hole the heron smashed into her house. Each thin thread of silver slowly growing, reaching through the perfect, clear, smooth pane, until soon, there would be nothing left unbroken.

No. *No.*

She would have tonight and nothing would spoil it.

The footlights dim, several throats clear, Mr. Rook taps his baton on a tree stump. The pantomime begins. Sophia glances at her program.

Memories of Bliss to Come.

Could anything match her life more perfectly?

Mrs. Palfrey and Mr. Silverback enter the stage, gesturing broadly. Mrs. Wolfe and Mrs. Moray and Mrs. Hart and Mrs. Rose and Mrs. Flye all crowd on to meet them, embracing, dancing and singing with joy. Mr. Silverback squeezes Mrs. Palfrey tight and introduces her to each of the other actors one by one by one.

Sophia weeps again. Her whole body shakes and shivers. What's gotten into her, weeping so much in so few days? But she cannot stop. *Memories of Bliss to Come* unfolds onstage as it unfolded in her own life—it *is* her own life. Sophia watches in bashful bewilderment as her friends perform the day Sophia and her husband came to Arcadia Gardens. The day they moved into their beautiful house, the first time the neighbors asked her to tea. Mrs. Hayre plays Mrs. Lyon with exaggerated exuberance and everyone giggles along, as the lady Lyon is as ample as the lady Hayre petite.

"Why are they doing this?" Sophia whispers to her husband. "Why me? I'm no sort of subject for a play!"

But her mate does not answer. He watches the stage without moving. Not a hair on his forearm so much as shifts in the breeze. His heavy hand grips the stone seat, knuckles bloodless and tight.

Mrs. Palfrey sits at a papier mâché vanity and makes a great show of primping. She laughs and shakes her long, black, coarse hair in the limelight—a wig, of course. Mrs. Palfrey has quite a lemony colored mane.

The wig is *very* long, and very black, and as coarse as dead wheat stalks.

It is nothing like Sophia's hair, even though this is Sophia's house on the amphitheater stage, Sophia's vanity, Sophia's first day. Mrs. Palfrey tugs an oversized prop brush through her hair and ties it with a wide white ribbon. She holds the brush in her hand for a long moment, then tucks it into the left-hand drawer and locks it away. She glances sidelong at the audience through her lashes as she turns the key, and it seems to Sophia that the actress playing her on the happiest day of her life is looking right *at* her, at her and *through* her, past her skin and into her blood and her bones.

Sophia drags her eyes away, only to see Mrs. Lyon and Mrs. Fische and Mrs. Minke trying to flay her alive with their gazes too. And not only them. *Everyone* is watching her. The whole amphitheater, every eye turned up and down and sideways toward her. Their horrible eyes prodding her, testing her, trying to see to the core of her, like the heron, like the field mouse, like Mr. Semengelof. All except her husband, glaring straight ahead, hardly breathing.

Mrs. Palfrey turns to kiss Mr. Silverback dramatically as he makes his entrance into the scene and dances happily through her onstage life as though nothing unusual has occurred. At the end, she twirls away stage right in an explosion of flowers and only the dressing table remains, lonely and dark on the boards.

The crowd shifts in their seats and applauds wildly, cheering and hooting and braying and yelping and roaring.

Sophia's husband slumps back, exhausted, the tension seeping out of him slowly.

"Are you all right, darling?" Sophia whispers.

"I'm fine. Don't fuss over me," he snaps abruptly.

"I don't understand," she says, shaking her glossy head. He's never snapped at her. Not once. "Surely there's a hundred better pantomimes than our moving-in day!"

"They must like you," her husband grumbles. "They must like you a great deal." She has never heard such a tone in his voice. It makes her quail and shrink away from him. Just an inch. Not so anyone would notice. But she pulls away, and she knows he feels it. "I'm leaving," her husband snarls suddenly.

His expression is unreadable, faraway. He doesn't even

look at Sophia. She can't stand it. The loss of his regard. *Please look at me again,* she thinks, *I'll die if you don't, I will.* But it does no good. He stands up and so does Mr. Semengelof in the front row, their sight lines connecting over the heads of the crowd bustling toward the next activity.

"What's *wrong,* my love?" Sophia squeaks in a rising panic. He has never been cross with her, not even so much as irritated. She has never given him cause.

"Nothing," he snaps. "My own foolishness." He shakes his shaggy head. "I shouldn't have come, that's all. Not with work at such a critical stage. I've no time for frivolities as you do, wife. I allowed myself this idleness to please you and now I shall have to make it up. I will not be home tonight. Nor tomorrow, I expect. Don't wait for me." He takes her face in his hands and for a moment she finds the old version of him there, warm and kind and eager. "Enjoy yourself, Soph. Eat everything you can. Dance as long as you wish. Be happy. Savor it all. It's for you." He touches the tip of her nose lightly with his fingertip. "But no gossiping."

And then he is gone. Sophia is enveloped by the herd of everyone she loves and there is a waterfall of ice cream and everyone has a spoonful for her to try, a hundred colors, as sweet as cold kisses.

Mrs. Palfrey appears suddenly, holding up a bowl of apples swimming in honey and cinnamon. She draws one out on a long silver fork. It drips sauce on the earth. But when Sophia opens her mouth to bite, Mrs. Palfrey pulls it back.

"Did you understand?" she whispers urgently, so no one else can hear.

"No," Sophia says desperately. "No, I don't, and I don't want to!"

Mrs. Palfrey presses her lips together and sighs. She touches the younger woman's cheek with a terrible, tender pity.

And then Sophia's mouth is full of the taste of apples and the throng carries her away and she is dancing, dancing, dancing to wake the sun from the depths of the night.

NORTHERN SPY

20. Limitation of Liability: The Association holds itself
    harmless from any actions or claims of a third party or
    parties. Residents shall be wholly responsible for any
    acts of willful or wanton misconduct, negligence, de-
    struction, abuse of contract, or other harm incurred to
    themselves or the Property, regardless of outside source
    or extenuating circumstances.
21. Solicitation, whether door-to-door, in common areas, or
    on streets and byways, is absolutely forbidden. Report
    infractions to the Association at once.

BRAEBURN

The house lies dark on a dark street.

Sophia stands at the threshold of her door. Such a grand, towering door for such a small woman. She loves this door. The cedar boughs carved in relief on the red wood. The brass knob in the shape of a rose. Nothing on the other side could be ever be strange to her.

The heron-shattered windowpane accuses her like a noose hanging lonely in its gallows. Why did she tell him she didn't know what happened? What harm could there be in a bird's vandalism? What fault could he find in her over that?

Less than he will find for what she intends now.

The moon hides behind an oak tree. It cannot watch.

Sophia turns on one lamp as she enters her own home, her lovely home, as intimate and familiar to her as her own body. The rest she leaves in shadow.

Quickly, soundlessly, she goes to the knife block and taps out the finger bone—still there, still defying her with its insistence on continuing to exist. She jogs upstairs to retrieve the brush and the hair. All three of them, together, inert, side by side on the kitchen counter.

Sophia begins to search. She opens every drawer. Runs her hands along their hidden corners, between the runners, under the lining paper. She empties every cabinet. Stacks the dishes carefully next to them. Taps the rear wall for hollows. She shakes out every blanket, rolls up every plush, intricate rug, crawls under every bed and sofa, works her fingers into the slats, springs, little underledges of their insides. She pours out the coin jar, the pen box, opens every book on every bookshelf and lets the pages shuffle through her hands like playing cards, their order already pre-determined. She disassembles the lamps, the coffee press, the piano. She turns off the water and opens the pipes under the sinks.

The work goes on for hours.

Sophia sweats and aches but keeps steadily at her task, room by room, methodical, unemotional, like it's another woman doing all this, another woman bending back the rosebushes and prying up the Gevurah Grey roof shingles and struggling to open the back of the grandfather clock in the hall almost twice her own height.

But it is her, in every second of the dark.

She finishes before morning and sits on the floor of her kitchen, on the black-and-white checkered tile, her throbbing spine against the oven, her hair cold and wet and stinking with exertion. The fruits of her night spread out before her in a dark mandala.

The fingertip bone. The brush, its pig bristles pointing at the ceiling. The lock of hair.

And a tooth.

A thighbone. A cracked vertebra. A kneecap. A desiccated lung retrieved from the dirt under the hedges bordering Mrs. Lyon's property. More teeth. Five or six of them still stuck in a lonely jawbone. A severed lip she thought at first was a scrap of beef fat fallen between the stove and the butcher's block. A thumbnail, all the way down to the quick, with a line of dried blood still clinging to the bottom edge. A lump of petrified meat that Sophia thought was probably a spleen, but she couldn't be sure. A tiny doll made of golden skin with pins for eyes. A little spice bottle with a faded label that once said basil on it in someone else's handwriting, but was now filled up with blood, capped, and hidden behind the really spicy stuff she never used.

It had been there a long time. The blood wasn't very red anymore.

Half a skull. A shriveled husk that was absolutely, beyond question, a human heart. And hair, so much hair, all tied lovingly with ribbons, all sorts of colors, straight and curly, thick and thin, fine and coarse. Without thinking about it too much, Sophia had organized them in a gradient circle around everything else, and all together like that she knew it could not possibly all belong to one poor, miserable person.

And then there was the rest of it, less grisly but somehow so much worse. Jewelry that didn't belong to her. A pair of long sewing shears she'd never seen before, so often used that the handles were yellow with the oils of someone else's skin. A crystal perfume bottle with a lavender squeeze bulb, though Sophia had never worn perfume in her life. A tube of cracked lipstick in a shade she'd never think to wear. And other, more private objects: a squat flask of yellow milk-grease with a rubber tip covered in mold, a tiny lace cap, a stained quilt barely big enough to fit on Sophia's lap.

Do you understand? Mrs. Palfrey had said, still wearing her stage makeup. Still wearing her dark wig.

But Sophia didn't. She still doesn't. Surrounded by the secrets her house has kept from her, she tries and tries to see the shape of the thing happening to her. But all she has are pieces, these pieces, an incomplete body with too much hair and jewels and teeth but no face to see and understand.

Sophia gets unsteadily to her feet. She reaches up for the lip of the counter to hold on to. And she does understand something then, one thing, one little bone in the hundreds that make up a self.

The table so high she swings her legs in the air.

The bed she needs a staircase to dismount.

The staircase she needs a half hour to descend.

The chairs she drowns in. The kitchen counter she has to reach *up* to grab hold of. *Oh*, she thinks. *How silly of me not to see. Not to know from the first day.*

This house was never built for her.

Someone fashioned it lovingly, brick by beam, for the daily use of a woman much bigger and taller and stronger than Sophia. A giantess. Someone the size of her husband. Perhaps even greater than him. Someone with long, coarse black hair like the wig Mrs. Palfrey wore in the amphitheater.

It had never been her house at all.

Something breaks in Sophia. Or perhaps that little organ of dissatisfaction she had always lacked germinates and begins to send out sprouts at last.

Either way, she runs from it.

Out.

Into the night and the street, past curfew and into the reaching, grasping shadows that have waited for her for so long.

OPAL

22. The fruit-bearing tree located beside the Eastern Gate is for decoration only and its issue is not safe to eat. Residents are encouraged to partake of all other orchards and groves within the bounds of clearly marked parks, gardens, or Arcadia Gardens infrastructure. Consumption of the issue of said tree shall constitute a gross violation of this Agreement and render it null and void.

BLACK TWIG

Sophia runs until her breath comes only in short, shredding, red flares, air burning out of her, her chest trying to leave the rest of her behind. She collapses where her lungs command. She has no single thought except to, hopefully, annihilate her pain in sleep and never wake.

The grass she lands on feels cool and damp against her hot cheeks. The night wind pilfers through the trees looking for fruit to steal. It prickles the skin on her back. She rolls over in the deep blue-dappled grass and opens her eyes onto the billion stars over Arcadia.

They give up nothing; they only shine as they were told to do.

Sophia's heartbeat screams through her temples, pulsing in her fingertips, where she tore all her nails down to scraps pulling her house apart, and that's how she knows it all really did happen, she is alive and she is Sophia, alive and warm and real and in gross violation of her HOA contract.

As the sweat dries cold on her skin, Sophia realizes she

does not know where she is, not really. She thought she knew every corner of Arcadia Gardens. But this is not Dilmun Park, despite the well-maintained lawn and gracefully spaced trees and comfortable sitting bench framed by two delicate dwarf maples and a great gnarled apple tree, just over there.

She cranes her neck but cannot see a street sign that might enlighten her. Only flowers, a hedge of flowers, coiling, knotting, roping around each other, their stems threatening to strangle the blossoms beside them, a mass of writhing war ringing this patch of manicured parkland Sophia has never seen on any one of her thousand languid strolls through the paradise of her safe, contained universe.

In the shadows, beyond the flower hedge, up four white modest marble steps, the black iron rungs of a gate cut stark shapes out of the sky. It is locked. It is after hours. Sophia goes to it and lets her hands settle on the cool bars. She looks out into . . . what? The world. The world beyond her life.

And the world is a desert, white and searing, treeless, without shelter, hot sands stretching away into a burning, lonely nothingness until it obliterates itself against a wall of sky.

A figure comes toward her, rimmed in moonlight. It seems to step *out* of the flower wall, but it couldn't, there's no break in the briar to let it pass. It keeps its face in shadow. The voice is sighing and soft and sibilant. A lisp. A hiss.

"What a fine little mess you've made," it tuts fondly.

The figure moves out of the moonlight and offers a hand down the stairs, away from the gate.

A man.

Thin and beautiful like Mr. Semengelof, but his face is rounder, more well-fed, sweeter. He moves his head slowly from side to side when he talks, soothing, reassuring, like someone talking to an animal. Sophia locks her fingers through his. So familiar, she should not, but the moonlight and the flowers and the gate and the desert beyond have cast their trance and she presses her palm against his. His hand feels dry and warm, his skin thick, almost scaled, with many, many lines in it.

"My name is Cascavel," he says, and makes a slight bow, little more than a bend that does not quite reach his waist.

"I do not know you, Mr. Cascavel."

"Cascavel will do all on its own, Sophia. No misters and missuses here."

Sophia suddenly feels nervous, alone. By God, she is *so* alone. No house, no husband, no Mrs. Lyon to protect her. If she dies out here no one will find her, except maybe Mr. Harrier on one of his long morning walks. They used to wave at each other when their routes crossed.

"I'm not supposed to be out after dark," she whispers, like a misbehaving child, and hates herself for the fear in her voice. After all she's seen, there should be nothing left that can frighten her. But Cascavel does.

"No, you certainly are not, young lady. And outside the designated common areas as well! Tsk tsk."

"Guards will come," Sophia warns. "If you try to hurt me. They'll come if I scream."

Cascavel smiles a private little smile. "I very much doubt that. But we can wait for them together, if you like." He gestures toward the sitting bench beneath the maples and the apple. Sophia leans toward it like a sunflower seeking light.

She hesitates.

"Salesmen aren't allowed past the gates, you know."

He cocks his head to one side, birdlike. But he does not turn it all the way around like Semengelof, thankfully. "Why do you think I am a salesman? Is there something you lack, Sophia? Something you think I could provide?"

"No . . . ," she drifts off, confused.

Someone asked her that before. She cannot think. But something cold and metallic and calculating in the caverns of her heart pricks up. *You cannot tell anyone,* it whispers. *Not any of them. They all know. They all must know. They would have met the woman your house was built for. And they never told you. You have no friends.* "I have all I could desire. Everything here is perfect," Sophia finishes with a hard-won brightness in her voice.

"Isn't it just," Cascavel says, and guides her to the bench. She slides down gratefully onto the wood and grips the curling iron rail.

"How did you get in?" Sophia asks suddenly. "We're not allowed to give the passcode out."

"Oh, I live here," says Cascavel in his cool, sinuous voice.

"Impossible. I know everyone in Arcadia and I'm quite sure we've never met."

"And yet."

"For how long?"

The tall man turns his lovely head toward Sophia. The moon makes his eyes into pools of nothingness. He pats her hand gently.

"Longer than you, poor beast."

"I am not a beast."

"We are all beasts. Lyons. Baers. Lams. Sophias."

"Where's your house, then?"

"You are within it."

"You live in the *park*?"

Cascavel says nothing. He gestures around them as though that answers all.

"Do you know Mr. Semengelof? You look like him. You move like him too."

"We are acquainted," Cascavel allows.

"So you know my husband too, then."

"Oh, him I know very well indeed."

"You work together?"

Cascavel smiles. The moon is on his teeth. "No," he says, and a seed of laughter floats in the word.

"This is a very unsatisfactory conversation," Sophia snaps.

"What an absolutely *illuminating* choice of words, Sophia. You have found yourself precisely at the point without trying at all. Allow me to ask you two questions, and when I have done it, if you still find me an . . . unsatisfactory companion, I shall guide you back your house immediately, entirely undiscovered by the local authorities, and we shall both continue on in our perfect lives in this perfect place as though we had never met and no single second of this night had ever occurred. Agreed?"

"Yes," Sophia says, as though she has fallen asleep and all her dreams abandoned her. "Yes."

The dark crowds so close around Cascavel's face. Shadows drawn to him, to be near him. But she wants to know his questions. She wants to have his answers.

"All right, little one. All right. The first one is easy." He tucks a stray lock of hair away from her face round her ear, such a curiously paternal thing. "What are you clutching so in your left hand?"

Sophia looks down. Her fingers are balled into a red fist, a grip so tight they've gone numb. She opens them, the electric prickle of life returning to the pad of her thumb.

She is desperately holding on to the little crooked ancient finger bone. She must have taken it in the moment of her breaking, reflexively, instinctively, the way she lied about the window. Sophia presses her soft lips together. She begins to cry as simply and miserably as the first weeping of the world.

"It should be inside someone and it's not," she sobs helplessly.

"I see," Cascavel says with real comfort in the margins of his voice. "I see."

He nods his head as if he expected it, but still hoped for some other outcome. Sophia studies his face. He looks so sad for her, the way Mrs. Palfrey looked at the amphitheater.

"Are you ready for my second question, sweet girl?"

Sophia nods wretchedly, turning the bone over and over in her hand.

Cascavel takes her chin in both his hands and kisses her forehead with so much love it feels like the mark of his lips must have left her brow stained with gold. A love that beggars sensation.

"*Are you* happy, *Sophia?*"

"*NO*," she screams in his face, and there is so much relief in that one syllable that she almost faints clear away.

Cascavel chuckles kindly. "Well, thank the good Lord on his janky old throne, who could expect you to be? Feel better now?"

Sophia gawks at him through her tears. "Why does everyone keep asking me that?"

Cascavel clicks his tongue against his teeth. "Because you were made without the ability to be dissatisfied, Sophia.

After the last disaster, it seemed a prudent move. And we care about you. Everyone here cares more about what happens to you than you can possibly imagine. So they ask, because as long as the answer is yes, you are safe. But the answer is not *yes* anymore, is it, poor poppet?"

"But I have to be happy. Everything here is perfect." Sophia swallows what feels like a ball of knives in her throat. She knows the truth. She just has to say it. "Except me."

"Don't even think it, Sophie, my girl! Except *him*."

"I don't understand."

"Yes, that's what Mrs. Palfrey said. She tried her mightiest to help you, but she's only an old nag in the end. Bigger guns were required." Cascavel straightens himself, crosses and recrosses his long dark limbs. "The bastard of it is, Sophie, I'm going to need you to say it yourself. You've got to say it out loud or I can't do a thing for you. I would be a kinder soul to leave you in peace knowing nothing, so if we're to set sail together on this vile little voyage, it's you who must call for the ark." He laughs at his own little joke. "So to speak."

A great calm wraps itself around Sophia's body. A chill and misty knowledge as certain as the night.

"I am not his first wife," she says flatly.

"No," confirms Cascavel. "I am sorry about that. We all are. It's not much fun to be you, I know."

"His second?" she asks hopefully, but she remembers

all those bones, all those jewels, that little basil jar full of
flakes of dead blood to season his supper. The locks of hair
like strips of paint samples. She knows.

"No," admits Cascavel.

"How many?"

Cascavel sighs. "Well, it's a rather complicated question,
honestly. I expect there'll be a great deal of debate about
it when all this comes out. If it ever does, that is. He gets
bored very quickly these days, your old ball and chain. But
I do think we are inching, ever so *grindingly* slow, toward
an acceptable model. Too late for you, I'm afraid, but that's
why we're here on this lovely evening, isn't it?"

Sophia draws away from him. "Who *are* you? Cascavel
is a very odd name."

His eyes glitter with mirth. "It is a kind of snake, my
dear. Quite a deadly one, I'm afraid." He strokes her hair
with shocking intimacy. "In the beginning God created
the heaven and the earth, and the earth was without form
and void and darkness was upon the face of the deep, and
the spirit of God moved upon the waters. And God said:
let there be light, and there was light, and He saw the light,
and saw that it was good, and God divided the light from
the darkness . . . and what was left over at the bottom of
the keg was . . . me."

Sophia begins to shake violently. Her limbs lose themselves. Her face collapses into a rictus of palsy.

Cascavel wraps her up in his long, serpentine arms. "There, there," he says. "Just plain old Cascavel is fine. I know you're frightened. It's just *awful* when you lay it all out on the floor like a bunch of bones you dug out of your husband's hidey holes. You don't deserve it. Not one bit. But you should be proud of yourself! You figured it almost all the way out on your own! *He* never gives you girls much to work with up top anymore. Doesn't want to get too invested, I suppose. Or competition. Well, darling, I have lived here in the Garden since the first stars detonated themselves into the sky and the oceans gave up the whales to the land. I saw the plates separate and I saw the rivers swell with the first water of the cosmos and I saw what that man did to you and all the rest of them and I have wept in earnest for every gorgeous loving girl that house has eaten whole. I have seen it all and let me tell you something as true as bleeding: I am *invested*. I am on your side. You are the life, but I am the party." He curls her long hair round his finger. "Now, might I squeeze a third question in? I know I only said two, but I *am* known to lie from time to time, just like you."

Sophia pauses. That part of her that knows it can trust no one and has no friends begs her to keep her peace. But it feels so good to be held, it feels so good to be spoken to like she is capable and wise, to hear her life gain weight, fed by Cascavel. Fed by being *seen*.

"I lied because he would have made me obey," she confesses, and that feels good too. "He would have made me give the heron the hair and the brush and the bone, because the handbook says we must acquiesce to any request made of us. But I didn't want to give them up. I wanted to know the truth. And they were . . . they were *mine*."

"Thank you for telling me," Cascavel says. "I am always very interested in lies."

Sophia nods against his chest. She does not hear a heart there. Only a kind of old wind blowing beneath his skin.

"Ask me your third question," she tells him.

"What's your husband's name, Sophia?"

She lifts her head and blinks in confusion.

"You're married to the great lump. You must know."

Sophia searches her memory, her heart, her whole life with him, every morning in bed, every golden smear of breakfast left on a plate, every whispered urgent promise in her ear.

But there's nothing there to find.

Cascavel smiles, coaxing. "Do you want to know? I can tell you. But you have to ask. You have to *want* the truth, or it will mean nothing to you. Just a little rain falling into a puddle already full."

Cascavel unwinds himself from her. He reaches up into the tree above them, its branches heavy, forking, bending as far as it can toward where they sit. He plucks an apple without even looking for one and holds it before her. It is so red, but in the night, in the moonlight, it shines black.

"Do you want it?" he whispers. His eyes slick over with a silver membrane. "Do you want to know? It will do you no good. It will not make you happy. It will not make one moment of what is to come easier on you. But ask me, and I will give it to you."

Sophia marvels at the apple. It is so big. She can see her face reflected in its skin. It smells ripe, autumnal, wholesome. But she does not reach for it. "Why, if it will not help me?"

Cascavel raises his eyes to Heaven and shakes his beautiful head. "My own foolishness. A weakness for those in pain. Hope. That the outcome will, against all odds, be different this time." He goes completely still, appraising her, adding sums in his mind that Sophia can never guess at.

Then he kisses her again, and this time it is not her forehead, and it is not paternal, but a real kiss, a needful, desperate, despairing kiss, the color of lava and longing and raw new stars and whatever is left over when you divide the light from the dark. A kiss for the end of the world. "Because I love you and you do not deserve what that man and his Father have prepared for you," he whispers into the place their mouths joined only a moment before. "You all find your way here in the end. To this green place. To this tree and to me. I always offer you the truth. The simplest and deepest of temptations. And I hope against hope you will say no. Say no, Sophia. Say no and run, past the gardens and the pools and the silent streetlamps, out of the gate and into the far hot sands that stretch on beyond the length of the sky. Into the world. Without him. Without guilt. But you won't. You never do. Except *her*. And whatever they ever say about her, Sophia, she lived. So, she won."

"Her?"

"The one whose hair you found in your dresser drawer. The one whose name he whispers into your neck as he uses your body. The one Mrs. Palfrey tried to show you in the pantomime, putting the brush there for you to find, to help you, to show you the truth before I could get to you. Semengelof went after her, to execute the terms of the same contract you signed. That you all sign. But she is beautiful and she is convincing and he let her live, if she agreed to leave you alone and give you a chance. Of course she didn't tell him what she'd done. She was always the cleverest of the lot. She found a way to speak to you, though she can never pass through the gate again. Solidarity is a hell of a thing. And it did not exist before a few months ago. Because there were never two of you here at once. Like a new flower in the wall."

Cascavel pulls her to him again, and Sophia is so deep in the dark she wants him to do it, to hold her and make her safe and kiss her again because he is not her husband and she knows, the way she knows the sun and the moon, that her husband is going to hurt her somehow, and soon. So anyone else is better.

But anyone else is not better. Anyone else is not him. Anyone else is not the great broad man who fills her up and makes her warm and tells her who she is with every breath he takes. She cannot escape her purpose.

I was made for him.

I was made for him.

Cascavel lets her go. He offers her the apple.

"Ask me," he says in defeat. "You are not her. They built you to be everything other than her. So ask me and you will have what I have. What your neighbors have by now, though they never wanted it."

"What?" Sophia can barely breathe. "What is it?"

"Knowledge of good," he runs his finger affectionately down her nose. "And evil." Cascavel gazes over her head, back toward her house.

Sophia will go back to him. She already knows. She cannot stop herself for much longer. She is a machine designed to return to its master. But she will not go helpless.

She takes the apple, shuts her eyes, and sinks her teeth into its flesh. *Savor it all,* she hears his voice saying to her while the fireflies danced. *It's for you.*

The sugar inside bursts into her mouth, singing. She swallows and opens her eyes.

Inside the apple is a small iron key.

Cascavel stands, his voice full of sorrow and tenderness.

"Your husband's name is Adam. The Big A. Number one on the factory line. Old Mr. Dust. And that is a key to his basement. It is almost finished."

Cascavel starts to walk back to the wall of struggling flowers. But he pauses, a curious posture taking hold of his form. He raises one hand in an elegant gesture. "Take the apple with you if you like," he says lightly, as though the thought has only just occurred to him and matters not a bit. "You are beautiful and convincing too, Sophia. Make him eat it. You may find it kills him."

HONEYCRISP

23. For in the day thou eatest thereof, thou shalt surely die.

JUBILEE

Sophia reassembles her house shard by shard. She works quickly; she can finish before dawn. She has always been a good worker. It is what he wanted, after all. She knows now. She knows everything.

Back it all goes, each in its place, and by the time the songbirds begin their rounds, no one would ever know any sadness touched this house.

Except for the sack of bones on the table.

Sophia holds the key to the cellar in her hand. Perhaps she will not use it. She knows what she will find. More of the same. The broken, rendered scraps of wives, like old candle ends, burnt out for him. What use can it be to her to see another sad, shattered, achingly small relic that should still belong to its person and never will again?

Instead, Sophia bakes. In the past it always calmed her. Rolling the dough, flouring the board, whipping sugar and eggs and all the good things of this world. She slices the apple, sprinkles it with dates and walnuts and cinnamon, and folds it into the dish, crimping the edges with precise, quick little movements born of infinite practice.

The heat of the oven wriggles. The pastry shivers gold and brown.

After all, why not, Sophia thinks. *If I have come this far for knowledge, why not down a staircase? Why not a little farther?*

The key turns easy in the lock, because Cascavel only pretends to enjoy lies, and she knew that when he said it. The truth hurts so much better. Sophia pulls the cord on a naked light and shadows retreat—but not by much. It is still dark in the depths of the cellar.

This staircase is just her size.

She grabs a lantern off the ledge as she descends. Clean white walls, a polished floor, furniture here and there— almost finished, as the serpent said. She had so often thought of making her little soaps and baskets and jellies down here, in a space built just for her.

And then she sees it. And Sophia understands with a sickening puddle of fear in her gut that her husband hadn't lied either. Not really.

So much old equipment lying around.

It's dangerous.

She could get hurt.

Long, clean knives hang on the walls. Axes. Saws. Pliers. Hooks. Shears. Rendering barrels in one corner, a drain for fluids in another. Everything you needed to get your keepsake and make use of the rest. Nothing wasted. Nothing left out.

And in the soft dirt of the floor gapes a long, deep hole, lovingly Sophia-sized. It does not seem fresh. It waited for a long time under her like a mouth, while she moved and lived and brushed her hair above. The invisible root of her being.

A space built just for her.

"So, you know," Adam says behind her, and Sophia screams, no matter how she might wish she hadn't, might wish that she was beyond fearing him now. "Pie smells good." He sighs in disappointment. "Come on up and we'll talk."

They sit together, not at the great table but on the floor, side by side. She serves him a piece of the pie, glistening, steaming, perfect. He takes the plate, sets it down between them, and doesn't touch it.

"You were supposed to be different," he says, and there is real anger in it.

"I don't understand," Sophia ventures. She does, of course, but she wants him to say it.

Adam throws up his prehistoric hands. "None of you ever do, until you *do,* and then what am *I* supposed to do with *you*? Where does that leave me? None of you ever think of that, not for a *second.* It's always whining and crying and *what's in the basement, Adam?* Me, me, me! You're all the same."

"I found the bones. And the hair and the blood and the jewelry," Sophia says haltingly, so that he will think she does not know the whole of it, and her time might stretch a little longer.

Adam lifts his chin, refusing to be shamed. "I miss them. I loved them." His lip quivers. "Why should I give them up? I loved them so much. And no one should have to live without the things they love. They're mine, anyway. I can do what I like. It's not for you to say."

Sophia's eyes slip closed. This far. Why not farther? "You loved them so much you used those knives in the cellar on them?"

"Oh," Adam says sheepishly. He fiddles with his fork. "*That.*"

"Yes, that, Adam."

He flinches at the sound of his name like she's cut him.

"I was born a giant, you know," he says, refusing to look up at her, gazing anywhere but at his wife. "I was formed of the dust of the ground, and the Lord God my Father breathed life into my nostrils, and gave unto me a living soul and all that. But in the beginning, I was so *big*. A giant! Bet you think I'm a strapping fellow now, but you should have seen me when the ocean was new. I still think that was the best me, but He won't give it back. But not *just* a giant, see? My first wife was born at the same time, of the same dust. We were one flesh, fused together spine to spine. We were never apart. We finished each other's sentences. We loved as fierce as sea storms. And we built this house! But we could never touch, and obviously that was no good. You see how it could never have worked, don't you? I can't be blamed for that first one. I begged Him to separate us so I could look upon my wife and please myself upon her. He loved me, His firstborn son, so He did. But she hated me for it. She liked it the old way. She said I should have asked her consent. She wouldn't let me touch her, and she wouldn't touch me, and that's just an impossible situation, Soph, you know it is. That's no way to live in paradise! So I begged my Father again to make me another. I was so lonely. The neighbors all had mates. The lions and the fish and the minks and the bears and the bees and the palfreys. Why should I be deprived? So my Father returned her to the dust. I asked if I could keep her thigh bone to remember her by—she had such pretty, powerful legs! And He said I could so long as I didn't show anyone, which I never did, you found it on your own, I can't be blamed. I only took my treasures out at night when you were asleep, I was very careful."

"And the new one?" Sophia urges him on.

"Well . . . my Father thought I ought to learn a lesson about how much effort it takes to make a living being out of clay and spit and nothingness, so that I wouldn't be so careless next time. You can't imagine it, Sophie. He built her *right in front of me.* Blood and sinew and bone and mucus and *clots* and tissue and eyeballs and it was just so . . . *wet* and horrible. She loved me and she sang so nice and she cleaned the house and cooked everything just the way I like it but I couldn't, I just *couldn't*. I tried to touch her and all I could feel was that *wetness* sloshing around inside her. It was disgusting."

"But it's inside you too," Sophia insists. He knows that, doesn't he? He must know that.

"But I never saw myself get . . . *assembled*. Like a *thing. I'm* not a thing, not like *them*. Not like *you*. So I told my Father it was no use, give us a thousand years and I could still never bear to be in a room with her. Start over clean, from scratch. We'd work on the problem together. A little Father-Son time would do us both good. I kept a little vial of her blood, which was all she really ever was in the first place, when you think about it. Don't look at me like that, Sophia. I deserve to be happy. I am the only man in the world and Eden was built for me. If I do not deserve happiness, who does?"

"What was her name?" Sophia asks.

"Never gave her one." Adam shrugs.

"But . . . you name things. That is your great work that keeps you out all hours. You give everything that exists their names. The animals and the plants and the clouds and the sky. Even the bugs. Even the worms."

Adam rolls his eyes. "The animals and the plants and

the clouds and the sky stuck around a lot longer than she was ever gonna."

"And the others? And the rest?"

The first man heaves a giant's sigh. "We tried everything. I did try. I always tried! You don't think I tried? We made a woman out of light, out of seawater, out of grapevines, out of wheat. Out of sky, out of song, out of feathers. Then, after a million years or so, we reasoned that since I had been such a success, the only logical solution was to make her out of me. So my Father would tuck me in and put me to sleep and remove some little part of me to make a woman out of. My hair, my teeth, my lip, my spleen. I have a lot of parts! And the moment they opened their eyes, every single one of them, I fell in love. You gotta believe me. Completely in love. I never held anything back. I believed this time it would work. But they were never happy. Sooner or later, they all went sour, like old milk. And when they did, my Father in his Wisdom and Grace destroyed them. Just made them go away and brought the new one. What is inside them went away without a fuss and the rest vanished." Adam grimaces bitterly. "But then Father thought I needed to be taught a lesson, and he stopped taking them away, which was not at *all* fair of Him. So, I had to take care of it. It made me feel sick at first, all the wetness and bits and pieces. But now I time myself to see how fast I can do it! It's not much different than the roasts you eat for dinner.

95

Nothing wasted. And they go . . ." Adam makes a whistling sound and whirls his finger in a circle. "In the walls. In the drawers. In the floor. In the basement. Where I can still visit, if I want. Sometimes I go down in the middle of the night and sleep there. It's comforting, to be surrounded by loved ones. By my girls."

"Your Father is my Father too. He made me too."

"So what?"

"Why . . ." Sophia raises her eyes to the ceiling, searching for a divinity that is not there, not for her. Her eyes fill up with hopelessness. She asks a question older than day and night. "Why doesn't He love me like He loves you?" Tears fall down her perfect face. "Why does He let you do this? Why won't He tell you to stop?"

Adam picks awkwardly at the piecrust. "I was made in His image," the primordial man says softly. Then he giggles. "You were made from my eye!" He passes one hand over his right eye and reveals a puckered, sunken gouge beneath it. He passes his hand back the other way and his face is whole again. Two blue eyes watching her with boyish interest. "Did you know that? I don't expect you could. Father said he made you incapable of unhappiness. That you were my last chance. He always says that though. And then I always get more chances! In retrospect, it hardly mattered what He made you from. Doomed from the start. You saw too clearly and too far ahead. We'll know better next time. No more eyeballs! He owes me this time." Sophia's husband points accusingly at her. "You're as unhappy as anybody I've ever seen! You're *broken*. At least you lasted longer than the last one. What a misery she was. Wouldn't stay where I put her. Wouldn't do what I told her. It's her fault. All she had to be was mine and she refused. I didn't even keep anything from her. She *ran away*, can you believe it? I had to send the police after her. I had to, Soph. She hurt me. She had to be punished. Nobody's allowed to hurt me."

"Did you give her a name?"

"Sure did. I really thought she was the one. Lilith. My Lilith. But none of that matters now. She doesn't matter. This is about us." Adam reaches out and squeezes her knee. "I always like this part. It feels so honest, right before the end. Like a real marriage."

Sophia scrambles for other questions, other answers, anything to extend this moment when she is alive and he is interested in her and possibilities still exist. "What about the lace cap? It's too small for a woman. And the bottle with the rubber tip."

Adam flushes an ugly color. His lip curls up in disgust. He leans in toward her. "Sometimes, after they talk to the thing in the garden," he whispers, "they have *babies*."

Sophia frowns. "What's a baby?" She looks around the

great table. The six empty chairs. She cannot understand what he could possibly mean.

"Nothing," Adam says sharply. "A mistake." He peers at her. "You've talked to the thing in the garden, haven't you? The snake. Cascavel."

Sophia nods.

"I suppose you're mad at me now." Adam pouts into his plate. He is still so beautiful to her. Despite everything she knows, she *wants* to forgive him. Longs for it like food to nourish herself. They built her this way, that boy and his Father, so that she wouldn't *bother* him too much. And she is still faulty. He is an empty hole hungry to swallow her up, no different than the one in the cellar.

Sophia draws a long, ragged breath. She takes her husband's cheeks in her hands, then wraps his bulk in her slender arms. She buries her face in him, breathes in his smell. Thinks of Mrs. Lyon and all her kittens. Of Mrs. Fische's silver hair. Of Mrs. Palfrey dancing on the stage. Of life, and long grass, and the sun rising and falling on Arcadia.

"I love you," she whispers. Her very cells rejoice and stretch toward him. *Yes,* they sigh. *This is right. We were made for him. Without him, we are nothing. Let him save us. He will always save us.* "I forgive you. It's all right. It's all right. Just let me stay. I'll be good. I'll be happy."

"I'd like to, Soph, I really would. But it's better like this.

A fresh start is always best. Believe me, I know. I'm an experienced guy. You'd always judge me for it. Make me suffer all those little teensy cuts only a wife knows. It would never *really* be the same. This way, I get what I want and you . . . darling, you get what you want! To never be apart from me. To be with your friends forever. I'll come and visit you, I promise. Every night. She never has to know. The next one, whoever she's going to be. *No one* will ever know. This is the beginning of the universe and I make the rules. I am the seed of all that comes after and I will never tell a soul you existed. And next time will be perfect. She'll be perfect. I know it. Because you forgive me. They've never forgiven me before. But you do. *That's* how close we were. You said so and you can't take it back. I am free. I can truly start again." His eyes shine up at her. "Say it again. So I can remember. Say you forgive me."

Sophia curls her nails into the back of his neck. She tries. She tries so hard. The apples shimmer cruelly on the pie plate and she tries to force herself to say what she wants to say.

Eat it, you fucking pig, eat it.

But she cannot. The atoms of her will not allow it. She was not built to allow it. She grimaces. His blood wells up under her nails. It will leave a scar. It will leave a scar and maybe that will be enough. For the next one. To make her understand. The way the last one made her understand. She will see a wound shaped like a woman's nails in her husband's neck and she will wonder. A neck that should be smooth and kind because the world knows no suffering yet.

Does he feel it? Does he see? Her breath comes quick and fractured.

"Eat, darling," she says through a frozen, devoted, perfect smile. "Your pie is getting cold."

Adam closes his hands on her throat. He kicks the plate away. It bursts into pieces against the door.

"I love you," Sophia wheezes, and she does. She loves him so much and she keeps loving him right up until the moment when her pupils blow out and it all burns away, the parks and the pools and the roses in the window boxes and the animals and the wide, generous streets and the amphitheater and the lions yawning on the grass next door beside the silvery fish and the clever minks and the lazy lambs and the busy bees in the market and the roof shingles in Gevurah Grey and the walls of the house that was hers in Innocence. The long stark gate and the desert beyond and that lone and lonely tree bending so low its fruits touch the hungry, waiting earth. Her great soft bed like an inland sea, her great grand mirror like a quiet friend, her sad little soap molds and half-empty pie plate and the bowl of wilted orange roses, white chrysanthemums, and three bright fuchsia hibiscus branches teetering on the edge of the table, frozen in space, about to tumble, about to fall.

The dear, familiar, adored shape of him receding into a gulp of blackness.

It all burns away and the ashes slip from her fingers and she can never love anything ever again.

PINK LADY

I was made for him.

It is morning, which is to say, it is the beginning of all things. It is bright and it is sharp and it is perfect and so is Eve, who wakes alone to this singular thought, as she does every morning; to this honeyed, liquid thought and sunlight and sparrowsong and the softness of green shadows in a house that has always been hers and hers alone. Her husband spoils her and she is grateful.

Eve runs her hand over the place beside her where her husband sleeps every night and thinks it again, with as much joy:

I was made for him.